Dedication

This book is dedicated to my children, whom I love so much—Daryl, Christian, Hope and Justice. May you all continue striving to make your dreams come true!

Special Dedication

Thank you to every student in South Florida and Atlanta, Georgia who has listened to my stories over the years. Your smiling faces and laughter encouraged me to share my stories with the world.

6

Do you have a baby sister? Well, I do, and her name is Penelope Price. She's as cute as any baby sister could be, but she sure cries a lot! She always has to get what she wants. Penelope's either trying to take my new toys Mommy got just for me or the juice I was supposed to have. I can't blame her though. When I was little, I cried sometimes when I wanted something too.

One time, I wanted chocolate crunch cereal for breakfast, and Mommy said it had too much sugar for a sweet little boy like me. Then, there was that Easter when I wanted to dress like a pirate, but she wouldn't let me. She said I had to wear a suit and tie, and I could be a pirate on Halloween. Who wants to dress like an adult? Yuck!

Every time Penelope cries, I remind her that she hasn't been around long enough to put up such a fuss. "Slow your roll," I howl. Nobody is going to get their way around here except me—big brother Pete, because I earned it. I'm the oldest! She just stares up at me with her large, watery, green eyes and keeps whining! Oh brother, here comes the waterworks again.

Mommy glances over at me and says "Petey Price, I've got my eye on you!"

For seven years, I made it through free and clear with very little trouble. But in the last ten months precious Penelope Price the Princess of I-must-have-my-way has been making my days much harder.

I turn to Mommy and howl, "I didn't do anything! She just keeps crying for no reason." Mommy bounces up from her seat at the kitchen table and swoops Penelope up from beside me. Penelope is drooling like a mad dog, and the disgusting slobber hits me right in the eye. Yuckity-yuck!

Drool is not cool! Mommy takes Penelope into the room for a nap. Finally, I can get some peace and quiet around here. I can play with my mega blocks and build the widest, tallest castle without Penelope crawling around and knocking the blocks down as she usually does.

"She's just a baby," Mommy always says. And nope, she never gets in trouble.

13

Later, Mommy comes out of the room with Penelope dressed in her perfectly pressed pants and hot pink shirt. Mommy says, "Petey, we will be back soon. Be good." And walks out the door before I can say, "Where are you going?"

While they're out Daddy helps me build my castle. He's just as happy as me to have peace and quiet. No Penelope! No Noise!

After watching a few of my favorite cartoons, I begin to wonder where Mommy and Penelope went. Did they go to the candy store, the park, or the toy store? They wouldn't go there without me, would they?

Penelope has been trying to bite, chew, and suck on everything that was not tied down to the floor. So at least while they were out, my blocks are not soaked in wet liked they've been washed up in a running river.

When Mommy and Penelope return home, I ask her, "Mommy, where did you go? The candy store? The mall? The pizza place? The movies?"

It had to be someplace good because Penelope is not crying anymore. She is so quiet. Did a wizard cast a quiet spell on her? It works on television.

"Was it a spell, Mommy?" I ask. "Why is she so quiet?"

Mommy laughs and shakes her head. She tells me that they went to see Dr. Smile. Penelope is finally getting her teeth.

"When teeth begin to grow out they push up through the gums. It can hurt a little bit," Mommy explains. "But Dr. Smile gave me some medicine for Penelope to soothe her gums."

"Dr. Smile said that Penelope will get her two middle teeth first then another and another," Mommy says. "By the time she turns three, she will have mouthful like yours. And she'll be able to brush her teeth by herself right beside you."

Maybe it's not so bad, I think to myself. As long as she never uses my toothbrush!

21

At night I visit Penelope in her crib. Her mouth is open a little, but there is no drool anymore, and she looks beautiful in her sleep. I can already see her little tooth poking through her gums. I lean against her crib and whisper, "Hey Penelope, I am sorry I got mad when you were crying.

I didn't know you were feeling pain. I just thought you were trying to be a pain. If it makes your gums feel better, you can drool all over my toys anytime you want. I still think it's disgusting, but it's okay. You're my little sister, and I love you."

I see her smile with her eyes closed. I'm not sure she heard me, but it feels good to tell her. While I watch her sleeping, Daddy appears at the door.

He smiles and says, "That's what big brothers do. We love our little sisters no matter what."

I look up and say, "Daddy, did you know Penelope has a new tooth?"

"Yes, and soon she will be able to eat all your favorite foods too," says Daddy.

Oh brother, I sigh. Or should I say oh sister? This could be a problem.

Comprehension Conversation Starters

Use these questions to begin a conversation about "Penelope's New Tooth"

1. Why did Mommy take Penelope to visit the doctor?

2. How does the medicine help Penelope?

3. Why do you think Petey believes he and Penelope will have a problem sharing food?

4. What would happen if Penelope does not like the same foods as Petey?

Author

Shanell Lee

Best-selling author Shanell Lee was born and raised in Clearwater, Florida. She grew up going to the beach and eating Italian ice. She loved living by the ocean so much she left home for more fun in the sun in Fort Lauderdale where she began her teaching career.

Shanell has four adult children and a beautiful granddaughter. She currently lives in Atlanta, Georgia where she serves as an educator. When she is not teaching children how to read, she is writing books for them to enjoy and ignite their passion for literacy.

Illustrator

Javier CL. (Mago)

Javier is a digital artist from Cuenca, Ecuador, with six years of experience as a children's book illustrator. He has collaborated with publishers, research centers and magazines. His illustrations have been exhibited in galleries in Ecuador and Canada.

He is the founder of the educational projects, Masters of Digital Art Ecuador and The Magic Exists, projects to help children without resources.

Javier also is character designer and content developer for animation, and the co-director of the short film "Hueso."

Interested in reading another book by Shanell Lee?
Check out Teacher, Teacher, What a Creature!.
This wonderful book can be found on amazon.com

Made in the USA
Columbia, SC
25 February 2022

56810369R00018

PENELOPE'S NEW TOOTH

Petey has a brand new sister. Her name is Penelope.
She's cute, but like all new babies she sure knows how
to cry and how to slobber!

She drools all over Petey's toys – Yuck! But what can
Petey do? Mommy always takes Penelope's side.
After all she's only a baby!

But maybe there's a reason why she's crying ...

Find out in Penelope's New Tooth – a story for all the
big brothers and sisters out there.

ISBN 9781070520940

900

9 781070 520940

Phoebe's
Extraordinary Wings

written by Rachel Janel

Illustrated by Moran Reudor